MW00913136

Tales Of A World Gone Bad

To Sharice:
Ms. Sexy Dwa
Continue to live your
your life and be
the sweet person
you are!
J. S. Walker

Tales Of A World Gone Bad

T.L. Walker

Copyright © 2009 by T.L. Walker.

ISBN: Hardcover   978-1-4363-8747-7
                Softcover   978-1-4363-8746-0

All rights reserved. No part of this book may be reproduced or transmitted in any form
or by any means, electronic or mechanical, including photocopying, recording, or by
any information storage and retrieval system, without permission in writing from the
copyright owner.

This book was printed in the United States of America.

To order additional copies of this book, contact:
Xlibris Corporation
1-888-795-4274
www.Xlibris.com
Orders@Xlibris.com
55118

Outline

#2

Anything Is Possible . . .

#3

Inspirational Spiritual (But do you believe?)

I would like to thank God for helping me and loving me, even when I didn't love myself. I would like to thank my grandmother for being a surrogate everything. Last but not least I would like to thank my biological mother. My childhood was a mixture of joyful times, as well as dysfunctional ones, that could have come from a Donald Goines novel. Throughout my life when my mother suffered from her addictions on some level, I always knew she loved me . . .

"Tales Of A World Gone Bad . . ."

Tales of a world gone bad . . . once upon a time in a foreign land lived a fortune teller.

He told people about their lives, by looking at their hands.

This one particular day a young man named Snow walked through his tent door.

Taking a seat in front of the man who called himself Amsterdam.

Snow wanted the man to tell him everything he could foresee.

Amsterdam took his hand and his nose started to bleed . . . all of a sudden scenes started to unfold.

He saw two brothers who were not very old.

One brother slayed the other one out in the field.

He saw people trying to build a structure to reach the sky.

He saw a man build a ark, afterwards a flood embarked.

The world was wiped clean.

He saw wars that were surreal, with weapons that would not stand still.

Metal balls flying through the sky.

Entire cities disappearing as millions died.

He saw famine that was so great . . . trying to jerk his hand away from this man, but it was to late.

The visions he saw seemed to live in the wake, of the man's eyes that turned into lakes of blood.

Surely this was death in disguise to deceive.

The man who held Amsterdam's hand said by using his mind, do you think I am a man?

I was bored . . . so I decided I would pay you a visit of sorts.

You realize if you die now all is lost. Your soul I can surely claim for you know not the Lord.

You couldn't even spell his name.

This soul snatching is so easy to do.

Just mislead the human and he will come directly to you.

I can see the suspense is killing you.

My name is Satan . . . how do you do.

Just at that moment the door to his tent blew.

A beautiful angel walked through.

Satan how many times must I tell you . . .

Michael this is none of your concern.

Satan turned his attention back to the man he was making have a heart attack.

Michael ordered Satan to let the man's hand go.

Almost at once Satan was thrown to the floor.

Michael walked slowly to the old man and began to tell him about God and his magnificent plans.

Michael gave the man a chance to decide, whom would be the one, to one day claim his soul.

The old man looked at Satan then to his new found friend.

Sir, tell we what I have to do, I want in . . .

Satan screamed in frustration.

Michael why don't you go back and let this one be.

I still have time left you know.

Michael helped Satan from off of the dirt floor.

Leave this place at once this round is lost.

Those are direct orders from the BOSS. Satan turned one last time to the man that would have done just fine.

If only he could have tricked the man with promises . . . that he would not have fore filled.

Michael spoke once more with his mind.

Satan if you don't leave at once . . . there won't be enough of you left to find.

At once Satan vanished almost into the thin air . . . it immediately started to snow everywhere.

Michael prayed to God to loose the man's tongue and revoke any curse that had been upon him.

Amsterdam became one of the saved.

He decided to pack up his tent.

His time could be better spent.

Michael seeing his job there was done, decided to go back to heaven to have a little fun.

Amsterdam traveled to and fro . . . telling everyone of the day Michael and Satan fought over his soul.

The things he had seen that would soon unfold, to a world that had yet to really be born.

Amsterdam while cozy in front of a open fire.

Started to write about all that had transpired.

Deciding he would need to keep track of all that would not allow him to sleep.

The first entry to his diary read.

TALES OF A WORLD GONE BAD . . .

#1
The Dark Side Of Life . . .

"Little Girl On The Streets . . ."

Thunder slashing through the sky . . . rain falling intensely in my eyes.

Looking all around me for a place to rest.

Deciding to just walk around clutching my belongings to my chest.

The streets are dark and I am alone . . .

Watching people go to their homes.

A few people notice my stare.

I continue to walk wanting to disappear.

Trying to decide what to do . . .

A car pulls along beside the curb.

I try to appear undisturbed.

The man driving makes it clear, that I have only to get into his car.

But BEWARE! ! !

Once I went about this deed, more then likely I will need . . . to sleep with him for a place to stay.

So life takes a turn this day.

Going from making A's and B's to sleeping with men as the weather drops to twenty degrees.

Sure enough the mood was set.

I get into his car . . . to avoid becoming further wet.

He makes small talk.

Pretending to care.

Once it is known I have no home.

He sees his plan set in stone.

Arriving back to his place . . . I am offered food.

Almost like we are in a race.

I take a shower so that I am clean.

He is already in bed.

He asks me to relax?

He asks me my age?

I feel myself being filled with a silent rage.

The lights go out.

I am afraid . . .

I feel this ripping pain as it sears through my flesh.

After it's over he allows me a moments rest.

I turn over and stare at the ceiling . . . in need of both physical and emotional healing.

"Wrapped To Tight! ! !"

Walking down a deserted street.

You chance by a youngster, you would like to meet.

So what the deeds you have in mind are sick, wicked, filled with malice.

Far from being kind . . . the workings of a lunatic.

Knowing the child is down and out.

That leaves little room for doubt.

You can easily out slick the naive one, onto the next one to be led astray.

Lured into a place of rest . . .

You promise the child riches if he or she would only but caress your chest.

One thing leads to another.

Now is the time you should be playing the role of big brother.

But . . . instead you take on the role of lover.

Man You Ain't Wrapped To Tight!!!

Rather then help out of the goodness of your heart.

You help due to being lead by another part.

After you've done the act . . . that turns little boys and girls into disillusioned men and women.

You send the victims on their way,

On to the next one to be led astray.

Now tell me . . . are these the actions of a man that's sane ? Or are these the actions of a man that's not Wrapped To Tight???

"Black Girl . . ."

Looking over my shoulder . . . I can't help but see, you strung out on drugs.

Hell! ! ! That could have been me.

Black girl where did you go astray?

Rushing from your parents house, because they wouldn't let you see Ray-Ray.

Was it worth it sister?

To be down and out.

Ray-Ray don't want you or he would have been about.

You were such a pretty child, too.

Black girl what happened to you?

I know you now, like I knew you when.

Don't make me tell your story of how it all began.

Long, long ago in a abandoned building, two oversexed teens couldn't stop that feeling.

A couple of hits here and there and then you were out.

Little did they realize that a life was on the way.

Kind of crazy how that happens, because just the other day.

You were by yourself, not a worry in the world.

Nine months later . . . your carting around a little girl.

Was it worth it sister?

To ruin your life, to make a situation worse.

He didn't even ask you to be his wife.

Raising your kid the best way you can.

She reached the age of sixteen, it started all over again.

The apple doesn't fall far from the tree, at least in this case.

Your daughter thinking she's grown decided to up and leave your home.

Living on the streets, trying to make ends meet.

At least she's with her man or so she thought, until it came to a swift end.

After he used her, he decided he didn't want her anymore.

Only one problem she was no longer the same.

You see her man left her with a habit.

Can you guess it's name?

CRACK! ! !

Black girl, sister what can I do?

I won't give you money.

You'll never see it through.

Another pretty child bites the dust.

What a waste!!!

Always in a rush.

How's it feel to be grown?

The same as when you were a child, but now you are all alone . . .

"Without So Much As A Cut . . ."

Sometimes I feel like anything could be.

>   At other times it's a struggle to just be me.

Seemingly coming through the hardships of the past.

>   Without so much as a cut, from life's looking glass.

Turning and tossing myself through.

>   A day mare a nightmare, too.

A uncertain future, that I cringe to think.

>   Like the Titanic is destined to sink.

Where can I run? Where can I hide?

>   As I gently stroke my crying baby's side.

I named wounded pride.

>   How much longer will my chance remain?

Coupled over in years of self defeated pain.

>   Buried so deep . . . it should never see.

The real inner being that is me.

>   I wimper in the recesses of my mind.

As I already know, I am running out of time.

>   Scratching . . . clawing . . . biting my way through.

The hardships of my mind anew.

"Daddy's Little Girl . . ."

Once upon a time, in a world with delicate morals.

Or so one would like to believe.

A woman didn't bare children, unless she was married.

Those who decided they would have children, without the father being there.

Would feel the bite of society you know where.

It just wasn't expected baring children, without a father in the nest.

Damn near every birth certificate in America read father knows best.

The woman who did manage to do the do.

The children were labeled bastards.

Thanks to you know who.

Not sticking around like he was expected to.

Daddy's little girl . . . survived without you.

Woman . . . Lady . . . Woman . . . Miss.

The next time you engage in sexual bliss.

Remember that any man can be a daddy.

But it's a father children tend to miss.

"Lessons Of Yesterday . . ."

All of your life you struggle anew.

Different situations that you must pull yourself through.

As you mature in age you find the world even more harsh this time.

You find that in your quest for love, you listened to a man who whispered like a dove.

Softly and gently into your ears.

Promises that are in fairy tales told for numerous years.

You listened to him as he wiped away your tears.

He feeds off of your basic need to be taken care of by a man such as he.

You become pregnant.

A unexpected event.

Your life is altered, your future seemingly spent.

You search for the man that opened your eyes to conceive.

That love was real and not make believe.

Due to different reasons unknown . . .

You find yourself all alone.

Reflecting upon the mistakes you have made.

Another mistake happens along, with a different face and a different name.

You listened anew to another as he whispers sweet nothings into your ear.

He is able to sense that your heart is in dire need of recompense.

Before long you find that you are once again with child.

The man that you thought was the answer to ever dilemma in life, tells you he can't marry you he already has a wife.

The same lessons continue to resurface their ugly heads, until they are learned well and put to bed.

Your future is not set in stone, if you were back in grade school and your teacher handed you back a paper marked wrong.

You would find the solution to the problem and simply move on . . .

Failing the test again would only leave you to blame.

You will constantly get the same lessons in life, until you learn.

They come in the form of a man.

Drugs that haunt you to the bitter end.

People that hate you because of your race.

Children taken away from you at birth.

Turmoil from supposed love ones that only value you for your accumulated worth . . .

How many times must you fail the tests of life, before you learn?

The lessons of yesterday will never simply go away, until they have been learned today.

"High School Daze . . ."

A big brick building located on a average street, in a black or white neighborhood.

You will surely meet teenagers in their prime.

Engaging in activities of crime.

Be it shootings on the third floor or be it knifings by the cafeteria door.

Sneaking around for places that best suit them for what they know could land them an arrest.

High school daze going up in a blaze.

It's no wonder they seem half crazed.

Engaging in blunts laced with crack, acid and smack.

I stand truly amazed that the children of tomorrow are battling the problems of today.

Becoming little young addicts.

Allowing their education to slip away.

Thinking themselves above things like just saying no! ! !

They do everything grown people do.

Have unprotected sex.

Have children by their ex's.

Try different and new drugs to feel important.

Losing themselves to the problems of today.

A bigger problem looms in the darkness, ready to take their lives away.

Be it by a drug overdose or years spent in jail.

I can promise you that their destined to live a new version of hell.

The one where all of your dreams crumble and you find yourself crying.
In a world that seems to self absorbed to care.

That you are now a junkie addict if you dare.

High school daze you don't need a sports figure or a president to tell you the harm that drugs can do.

You need look no further than a family member or a friend.

Struggling with drug addiction to the bitter end! ! !

"Misty Eyes . . ."

Why do you cry Misty Eyes?

     Crying over a way of life that's slowly bringing about your demise.

Daily you travel to the stars and back, as your infant child cries for similac.

     Placing the rusty pipe to your ever dry mouth.

Is there any wonder why your life has gone down south?

     Misty Eyes . . . can you focus on something new, besides a little white rock, that's killing you.

     How can you solve the problems in your life?

If the only time you are sober is to turn a trick at night.

     Ignoring the blessings that are bestowed upon you.

Your child was born healthy . . . no thanks to you.

     You haven't overdosed, even though you've come close.

Misty Eyes . . . why do you cry?

     I'm beginning to think everything you say, about wanting to get clean is a fake, as the spray you use.

     To try and cover the smell of the crack you abuse.

Misty Eyes . . . your no stranger to life.

     You've been around for awhile.

That's right! ! !

Your no babe in the woods.

Misty Eyes . . . when you had a child, your life ceased to be your own.

Everyday you live is another day you could die, from the big white rock.

That makes you . . . Misty Eyes.

Reflect upon a life besides your own.

Wise up . . . leave that crack pipe alone! ! !

"The Guise Of Your Lonely Eyes . . ."

The moon takes on the guise of your lonely eyes.

Sadly in search of your family . . . surprise! !!

How many years must go by, before glancing, upon your innocent face?

Soon your little face will be erased.

I sit back and wonder, if you have fallen, into the clutches of death.

Breathing what can only be described as your last breath.

I shall be haunted forever and a day.

That you were born, into a life which is being played out, in this way.

At the mercy of a addict mother that seems not to care.

Just as long as her drug supply doesn't disappear.

Your so young . . .

Your so brave . . .

Yet your life is full of pain, from the one that is enslaved.

"Dancing In The Mist Of Evil . . ."

Walking through the darkness of night.

 Seeking the reason I must continue to fight.

Knowing evil looms about ready to take flight.

 Hiding in a vaporous kiss.

One by one my defenses fall.

 I know so much . . . yet I know nothing at all.

Dancing in the mist of evil.

 The world ceases to make sense.

I search my heart and mind for repentance.

 I find no peace.

Forever at war.

 With myself and those who come knocking, on my door.

Dancing in the mist of evil.

 Slowly running out of breath.

I glanced across the once crowded room.

 Finding myself face to face with death! ! !

"Are You There Yet . . ."

Are you there yet asked the son to the mom?

    Are you at that point you can no longer go on?

Do you crave it so bad you can't see?

    Is it worth you losing me?

Have you lost enough places to stay?

    Are you through selling your welfare away?

Will you actually provide decent clothes for me to wear to school?

    Will you be home when I wake up and it's half past two(am)?

How many nights must I see numerous people passed out off of drugs?

    But do you listen when I scream?

No . . . No . . . No.

    Are you there yet?

If you could but only think of me.

    I am but the child you allowed to be.

I love you mommy.

    No matter what horrors you have put me through.

All it takes is one time and you could be no longer amongst the living.

That drug you love won't love you back.

You continue to live another day.

God is giving you a chance to get clean and make something of your life.

But you continue to throw it away . . .

"Puff Goes The Dragon! ! !"

Puff Goes The Dragon! ! !

    In all his splendor and grace.

You become entranced.

    Slowly building up the much needed strength, to ask the dragon to dance.

Knowing your life has now been taken from your hands.

    Puff Goes The Dragon! ! !

What have I done?

    Upon touching him, I thought it would be fun.

Once he grasped my hand.

    The lights went out, all across the land.

I began to shiver.

    I began to cry.

The dragon leaned closer and kissed me, as I began to die.

    Puff Goes The Dragon! ! !

Once, twice, thrice.

    The dragon has other names, that aren't quite so nice.

Crack, Smack and Heroin, too.

The dragon uses other names, disguised as your friend.

Most often then not you become inclined to let him in.

Puff Goes The Dragon! ! !

As you hit the floor your heart has burst, in your chest.

You are no more. The dragon leaves, in the same manner, in which he came.

In a cloud of smoke.

Crack, Smack and Heroin.

Being his name . . .

"Little Butterfly's Gonna Die . . ."

Wakeup!!! You've been doing this scene for to many years . . .

Shutup! ! !I regret ever acknowledging your tears.

Wiseup! ! ! This is the dawn of a brand new day.

Little Butterfly's Gonna Die . . . if you persist on living your life this way.

So many decades tried and true.

Yet you continue to do that thing you do.

Falling further and further through . . . a drug hazed, late on rent phase, depending on crack daze so that you may exist to die, maze of depression and fear that hide away, in your mind.

Baby girl you are running out of time.

Little Butterfly's Gonna Die . . .

Mark my words as my tears begin to fly an unmarked course not meant for my eyes.

Seeing your life . . . seeing your slow demise.

Little Butterfly's Gonna Die . . . unless you open them eyes.

Wide and realize death is standing vigil by your side.

In the form of CRACK!

The one you love to hide . . .

"Whatever Name I Go By . . ."

Smack! ! !

Crack! ! !

Whatever name I go by . . .

Your still getting in line.

Ready to buy.

Lying! Cheating! Stealing! Beating!

Knowing your children barely eating.

It's all the same to you.

Cause all you care about is what you do! ! !

Sniff! Smoke! Shoot! Choke!

Wondering who you can get next to buy you dope?

Burning bridges everywhere you go . . . family, friends, one night stands, Johns, pawns whomever you can work your charms.

Death going into your veins.

Slowly but surely driving your ass insane.

"Looking For Love . . ."

Looking for love . . . any and everywhere it seems.

Unable to realize your deepest dreams.

Looking for love . . . in the vibration of a man's baritone voice or in the dress size of your woman of choice.

Little did you realize that you are your greatest prize.

First make sure your emotional circle is complete.

That your not a mental wreck . . . void and depleted.

Before rushing into love so to speak.

Looking for love . . . but finding only pain.

It seems your love has been given to plenty in vain.

They take pretending to adore, they promise you dreams that are forever more.

Devices in which to manipulate, so that for the time being, you both can relate.

You both get your hearts desire, until one of you realizes.

That your looking for love . . . that starts from within.

Once you love yourself, only then can you begin, to love your fellow woman or man.

"Pull Her Coat . . ."

I have the urge to pull her coat to the fact.

That her down low man ain't all that.

But sister to sister if I were to proclaim . . .

That her man goes from woman to woman just the same.

While he is with his lady "T" he is still trying to sex everyone else including me.

He thinks he is the personification of a real man.

I no longer wonder why he has yet to taste real love.

If you are in a relationship where there is love for the other person, no one should be able to creep in.

If home girl could only understand . . . it is not with jealousy that makes me wish to open her eyes.

It is because of my ignorance I was forced to become wise.

Giving him the benefit of a doubt, because facts I did not have . . . nor did I find out.

That dude was and is like a serpent crawling along a tree.

I didn't find this out until it was to late for me.

He tells lies without a trace of moral fiber, but with ease and sometimes grace.

Always a answer to make you second guess, your intelligence you had long
   sense laid to rest.

It's not my place to pull her coat, as I continue to smile.

   Continue to think you are the only one.

Life will pull your coat, before it is all done!

"I Hear You Call Yourself A Man . . ."

I hate the power that resides in the swiftness of your closed fist.

I hate the power you have to dismiss.

I hate the way you make me feel as if I have no pride.

I hate the way you have the power to make me feel useless inside.

I hate the way you have the power to make me want you.

I hate the way you have the power to say we are through.

I hate the way I am just your sexual pleasure, but what can I do.

I hate when I come close to that heart of stone, when any real emotions surface through, I am immediately erased.

I hate that you have the freedom to come and go.

I hate the fact your approval I will never get and the importance of it you will never know.

I hate how you judge me by my face.

Your mouth starts to water and you already want a taste.

I hate the fact that you tried so hard to get me for your own

As you tried equally as hard to get o
a better being than they had ever known.

I hate the fact your heart can never

I hate the fact that even when you call yourse
lying.

I hate the fact that you are forever preaching, about how you want a good
    woman by your side.

    And when you get her you keep a extra piece to satisfy your pride.

I hate the fact that if you take a woman out to dinner, you believe you have
    just earned your right to her bed.

I hate the fact that your heart is so corrupt, you actually believe every lie you
    ever said.

    I hate the fact that you would kill another man if he treated your
mother, in such a way.

    Yet you live like this everyday.

I hear you call yourself a man . . . when in actuality all you are is a dressed
    up trashcan! ! !

    Standing out everywhere you go, yet full of trash from head to toe.

"Searching For Love . . . Finding Only Despair"

Searching for love . . . finding only despair.

In the haunted eyes of those that pretend to care.

In a endless cycle of mental abuse, neither party willing to cut the other one loose.

Everyone's seeking their unrealistic dreams of their envisionment of love, as it would seem.

Always reaching forth as true love pulls away.

As elusive as the dawn of a brand new day.

Searching for love . . . finding only despair.

Leaning towards a life where you only pretend to care.

The real thing can not stand in the wake of lies and cheating.

So let's be real with ourselves.

What type of relationship do you really want to be in?

"Betrayal Of The Heart . . ."

The taste of acid . . . bitter and placid.

Betrayal of the heart . . .

Was it really love destined from up above or was it just something to start?

Often in our quest for a love in which to rest, we find ourselves victims in a chest match.

Slain by a action, caused by a attraction.

What is to become of us?

Do we simply fake the moves of late?

Betrayal of the heart . . .

How does one prevent the heartache?

Is there a path in which to take, so that we never know hurt?

The pain so deep, you find you can not sleep.

Often revisiting places where the imminent chase began.

Betrayal of the heart . . .

Going through the metamorphosis of change, either you decide to hurt as many people as time would allow.

Or you decide to get even with the one that hurt you somehow.

You walk around carrying your heart in a cage.

When someone get's to close, your heart becomes enraged.

Jumping from side to side.

Determined not to fall victim to the ride, otherwise known as love.

Be it the real thing or a test drive swing.

The pain felt after someone else has dwelt.

In the arms you thought you knew, having been engaged in time exchanged with the love, thought only for you.

You have since learned, once you have bitten into the fruit of love.

There is no way of telling if you will be burned.

Betrayal of the heart . . . a lesson constantly being learned! ! !

"My Pain Rings Silent . . ."

My pain rings silent, my pain rings true.

> A noise so vast.

It can only be heard by you.

> A pitch so high.

That to those passing by it's silent.

> I don't recall that over the years, if I have even shed genuine tears.

My entire being is numb.

> Swallowed whole.

A eating breathing, sleeping corpse existing is my daily remorse.

> I constantly wonder . . . why?

Why does one need to feel such despair?

> I'm all dried up inside.

To the general passerby.

> I meet the requirements to the naked eye, but to the man up above.

He sees the real heart and soul.

> My pain rings silent, my pain rings true.

A noise so vast, it can only be heard by you.

The one who resides up above.

> Repair me Lord for I am the soilest of doves.

"Who Loves You Baby?"

Lending out your body for stolen pleasures, in the night.

Searching for companionship, even though the sex doesn't feel right.

With a lonely heart you allow yourself to take risks.

If your not careful your body will catch more than a caress and a kiss . . .

Who loves you baby?

Because it's ovious it's not the man you are with.

Because it's ovious it's not you giving away your gift.

Because it is ovious it's not the world all you feel is the cold.

Who loves you baby?

As you drink your rum mixed with coke.

As you fail to use a condom, finding yourself semen soaked.

As you fear this could be the oneday you carelessly gave your life away . . .

Who loves you baby?

As you secretly cry in your pillow at night.

Knowing how your living just ain't right.

Your alone . . . a walking wound before you even allow yourself to heal.

The scab is pulled away once more.

Who loves you baby?

Are you ready to discard that label . . . whore?

"Don't You Know . . . No Good"

Sometimes I feel your presence looking from, behind my eyes.

I feel as if your spirit is trying to fight mine.

I find myself laughing, sometimes it feels and sounds like you.

I find myself doing things you would do.

I find I am always a half a step, away from your mistakes of yesterday.

Don't you know . . . no good?

I find myself jumping from relationship to the next.

It would seem you and I have not had a good time with love.

I never had any man care, if I lived or died.

I only had the men creeping and messing with my self esteem.

Never the bride . . . always the bridesmaid.

Never the woman . . . just the little girl being played.

You fell into the drug trap, to handle your pain.

I fell into the sex trap half looking for a father and partially going insane.

I wanted to feel normal and do things that other people did, but the streets were far from being kind.

Imagine drinking, until you can't remember today or yesterday.

    Just meaningless relationships with men.

Throughout your troubled life . . . you managed to get out of the street game
    in time.

    Me on the other hand I didn't know how to play.

I didn't know I was standing in quicksand.

"Ice Cold Existence . . ."

This here is my life . . . can you guess my profession?

I work late hours way into the night.

I guess you can say I'm partners with the graveyard shift alright.

Walking the cold streets . . . no matter what time of year.

My feet be killing me, but I can't allow myself to care.

I be wearing the sexy outfits, that show my every thought.

And if you look even closer, into my eyes, you'll see every battle I ever fought.

I live a ice cold existence . . . for every man I allow to touch, my body a thank you is never enough.

Cold hard cash is all I understand!

My heart isn't for sale, it's my body that's in demand.

I'll walk these streets, until I'm to old to deal.

When my body starts to tell my real age.

I'll have no choice, but to step down from my career choice, while I'm still all the rage.

Afraid???

Naw ! ! ! I ain't afraid! ! !

You see I've been a walking corpse for years.

Now all I need is a grave . . .

"A Cry In The Wild . . ."

A cry in the wild.

　　My thoughts resembling that of a small child.

Life meaning nothing more than cruel fate.

　　My eyes hide pools of liguid hate.

Nothing ever being what it seems.

　　Nothing manifesting from my magnificent dreams.

Thoughts crashing on the highway to success.

　　Landing in a heap of nothingness.

My way short of poor.

　　The world gets ahead using a magic door.

Trust being nothing I know.

　　My fingers have that look of hard work about them.

My face well worn before my time.

　　What oh what is my crime?

To have a heart that never truly worked.

　　To only encounter men that were whores or jerks.

To never know what it is like to be someone's mom.

　　To fall victim to deaths seductive charms.

"Waking Up For The First Time . . ."

One day I woke up as usual and I felt so cold . . .

I scratched my head, making my way to the bathroom.

I looked into the mirror and realized I was old.

Time had ran away from me, like a thief in the night.

It had stolen my youth so fast there wasn't time to fight.

I was never comfortable in my own skin.

Never really interested in attracting all those men . . .

I had always wanted to be in a exclusive relationship.

To have a man to call my own, instead I would get other women's men by loan.

Nine times out of ten it was because they lied, saying they were single, even though their wife just gave them a ride.

The other one percent was a matter of my pride.

I always tried to play fair, in a world of contenders who barely even cared.

I allowed men to abuse my spirit from within.

If you can't beat them, join them.

How can one win?

For one thing your not supposed to give in.

If a relationship you are in goes against everything you are . . .

Newsflash you don't need it by far.

If your messing with a man that's claiming he's single . . . yet you know differently at a half past ten! ! !

Start thinking with your mind and not your heart. Unless you want to end up like me . . .

Used, abused, old and can't half see past all the turmoil I allowed to happen to me.

Out of all them men that wouldn't stop sniffing my way.

In the end I ended up alone . . . not even my self respect would stay! ! !

"I Ran Out Of Time . . ."

Run silent . . . run deep.

Is the pain as it began to creep.

Through my veins like a early morning snore, as I wipe away the last traces of evidence that once labeled me a whore . . .

My past always biting at my heels.

My remorse forever heavy as it spills forth from my cup.

Runneth over . . . say no more . . . I chose that path.

Seemingly a lifetime ago.

Knowing life but never having felt it's bitter cold.

As my lips cracked . . .

As my belly ached . . .

I put aside my soul for nights without break.

I felt the need to make it own my own.

Believing myself to be all grown.

I was soon taught what being grown really was.

Let me count the ways as I continued to write the script of my life's disturbing page . . . after page.

My life ended like a badly thought out crime.

Never did I once think it through carefully.

As it was to late for I had ran out of time . . .

"A Mirror Where I First Viewed Death . . ."

I see my image in a mirror and I frown.

    For over the years my looks have swiftly went down.

I leave my apartment . . . as I take a stroll to the neighborhood park.

    I hear a whistle coming from the dark.

I turn my head to and fro with a start.

    My thoughts racing across time and space.

My life had nothing to show for it.

    Could it be a waste?

I never produced life from my womb . . . reason being I never found a man, in which love could bloom.

    I brushed my hand through my short hair, allowing my hand to caress my face.

    Heaven help my youth . . . I've seemed to have misplaced it.

Streams of gray intermix with my brows.

    I am by myself the same as in my youth, but now I find myself encased in buckets of fear.

    Inching closer beside me as I take a rest.

The coldness of the park bench is ignored.

A brittle tear finds it's way down my face, as the cold enters through my feet.

Bitterness encases my heart, as gloom holds me near.

My body grows numb, as a beautiful young stranger takes a seat next to me.

I asked him what was he doing out all alone this late?

He told me he was expecting a date. I responded that I didn't catch his name.

He said in any language it could be pronounced the same "DEATH".

What a quiet elegance it gave to any room.

I told him I needed more time.

He just shook his beautiful head as love shined brightly, in his penetrating dark eyes.

He simply replied "Why?"

Your whole life you've been dying.

Never having taken advantage of a precious gift.

Now you no longer have a life to live.

As he enveloped me with a tender kiss, he spoke to me mentally.

Death transformed into the father I never knew.

The love with a man that never came true.

As he broke the kiss . . . he peered deep, into my eyes.

I gasped out my life's essence having savored the saltiness of his kiss, a tingle traveled the course of my spine.

He held me then . . . so gently as I was crying.

He loved me so sweetly . . . as I was dying.

In death I found the peace that life could not give.

In the throws of death I found the courage to live, but my time had run out.

And all that was left . . . my now empty apartment and a mirror where I first viewed death.

#2

Anything Is Possible . . .

"African Prince . . ."

African Prince so strong and brave.

You existed once, before you became a slave.

You conquered tribes to and fro.

Little did you realize, that betrayal was awaiting you, with every beat of a tribal drum.

African Prince what can I say.

For your greatness is now, only a memory to this day.

I can only cry with anguish in my heart.

For what remains of the great African Prince couldn't fill up a ark.

African Prince so strong and brave, due to the greed of your fellow men.

You arrived at a early end.

Just when you realized your place in life, your status changed from king and queen, to cotton picker and midwife.

African Prince what else can I say?

Due to the deeds of the past, our race has been turned, every which way.

King, Queen, Nigger, Spade.

These are but a few names that have come our way.

African Prince listen to my call.

Your greatness still remains, it's just wounded that's all.

If you listen to the cries of the world.

Blacks ain't no good! ! !

Send their asses back to Africa we should! ! ! The only good nigger is a dead nigger.

Then yes you are already dead.

For success must first originate, fiom within your head.

Knowledge is the key.

Determination is the way.

You are what you think, you feel what you say.

And if you think you are a nigger, then you will remain that way . . .

"The Cries Of A Slave . . ."

Working until the sun goes down.

Everyday a new misery can be found.

Never knowing if this will be your last day with your family, before someone is sold away.

The cries of a slave . . . won't go away.

It's hard to just pretend to be content with the bounds of slavery.

Being forced to make the lives of those whom enslave a ever continuing maze of happiness.

While you try to not meet a early grave.

Tending to the clothing of the Mr. and Mrs.

Pretending to respond to the master's kisses.

The cries of a slave . . . running through the woods, during different times of year.

Searching for the north, just wanting to disappear.

Needing hope. Only finding despair.

Not content to go through life as a cotton picker, a butler or midwife.

The evil that men do is astounding but all so true.

The institution of slavery.

Blacks being treated like pedigree.

The only worth to be found is in the manual labor, that came tumbling down,
from the bone weary limbs of the oppressed.

While the master usually feeling pride swell deep, in his chest.

Looking over all his accomplishments in life. Feeling proud he caught
him a beautiful wife.

Not giving his slaves a thought in hell.

The cries of a slave . . . known so well, being carried in the capable arms of
the wind.

The enslaved remorse over the nightmare within.

When a loved one was murdered cold.

What could a slave do?

The atrocity that was bestowed upon the young and old.

Beloved slave.

So determined to make their way in a world that controlled their every move,
until their dying day.

Oh! Lord forgive them for they know not what they do! ! !

The cries of a slave . . . can you hear the pain in their voices?

I do . . .

"Racism Still Lives . . ."

I notice the frustration, on your face.

Of well made plans often erased.

Thinking of the past and all your eyes have seen.

I wouldn't be shocked if our race was embittered and mean.

There are a few of us that reside in hate, but for the most part we can relate.

To what our ancestors have been through and for that reason alone we mistrust.

But we don't hate you.

Hate is to strong a emotion.

One that ruins lives.

Hate is worse than cancer.

Promised to bring about your demise.

To every African American who decided to hate.

Realize what era we stand in.

The brink of the year 2010.

What kind of people in a whole would we be?

If we still have unresolved issues from the 18th and 19th century.

We can build a rocket to land on the moon, yet we can't stop hating each
    other.

    That sounds like a people that's doomed.

We put up huge fronts against other nations, yet it's our own nation on the
    verge of separation.

For every heart that rents out rooms to hate.

    Be careful that the tenants don't converge, upon you leaving nothing
left in their wake.

"A Soldier's Welcome . . ."

Fighting for years for something resembling respect.

African Americans most likely lacked.

The aspect to pick what they would prefer to do.

They decided to carve a way for themselves.

Upon the news that a war was a brewing.

Enlisted into every branch that would take.

A black man worth his weight.

Fighting in World War II.

Blacks dying.

Racism frying.

The remains of common sense.

Racism the prodigal fence.

That no matter how many black lives were lost.

Fighting for what is considered an American cause.

Still didn't make the unrealistic see.

If our blood was good enough to shed, for a country that until recently turned it's head.

Seeing us as niggers born and bred.

Fit for cotton picking.

Decisively better dead.

Yet when it came to seeing us as we deserve to be seen.

Not as unintelligent animals, but as human beings. The world . . . more importantly the America that we have earned the right to call home.

Still is a enabler for racism to roam.

A soldier's welcome . . . is forth coming indeed.

Not that other lives lost were not as valuable to the creed, of being a soldier and helping our country be.

The envisionment of what our ancestors could see.

Something that has been lost over the centuries.

We've only touched upon the tip of what makes us, in our quest for greatness.

We must first dream, before we can make it a reality.

All the more prolific in it's being.

We must know the mistakes of before.

The past has a open door, which allows elements in time.

To revisit the hearts of you and I.

To see what we would do.

When being confronted with something so true, as the basic teaching of
Christ:

"But I say unto you, love your enemies, bless them that curse you, do
good to them that hate you and pray for them which despitefully use you
and persecute you."

"The Soil . . . The Ground . . . The Fight!!!"

Pssp . . . stop what you are doing.

> Listen! don't make a sound.

Look down at where you are standing.

> The soil . . . the ground . . . the fight.

Look to your left and look to your right.

> If you are black you are taking a lot for granted.

As a people if we don't take advantage, we individually are to blame.

> Open your eyes and see for the first time.

Slavery was a way of life in 1859.

> Blacks were still being lynched in 1968.

We may be in the 21st century, but are we lined up at the charging gates?

> For all the aguish that has come our way.

Have we really taken advantage of what came, from the struggles of yesterday?

> If not we are throwing away our progress without even trying.

Now is not the time to slow down.

> If I can still walk into the ghetto and pick out every stereotype come to life.

We sure as hell aren't doing right.

So many of our people are content to live out their days, in a dysfunctional maze.

Always trying to blame the white man . . . you better wake up fast.

The time is now! ! !

Don't settle for less than what the fight has struggled for . . .

"A Free Beings Nightmare . . ."

As I laid in my bed.

I shut my eyes and all was right.

Sleep came upon me quickly this night.

This dream takes me to another time and place.

1860 South Carolina my heart begins to race . . .

I look around me and as far as my eyes could see, nothing but land and dark faces staring back at me.

Looking down at my hands I gasp out loud.

Oh! Lord what has happened to a people so proud?

Tattered clothing from head to toe.

I'm standing in the midst of a cotton field.

The slaves snow . . .

I stand still utterly amazed.

I try to conjure the strength to be brave.

I watched the other slaves pick cotton.

Some were so old they could barely make it through, while others sang a negro spiritual or two.

Seeing a white man sitting upon his horse.

I began to pick cotton.

My fingers were being ripped.

I halted my actions.

My head began to ache.

I looked around me for a immediate means of escape.

The sun singed my very brow.

I felt as if I were going to go crazy, as the other slaves whispered I was lazy.

As I started to run, I arrived at the master's home.

It smelled of money, a place where power roamed.

The house servants were all light complexioned, mixed heritage already a reflection of the times, in which they lived.

I was grabbed at once and told to go upstairs to the master's bedroom.

Once there I knocked twice . . . I was told to come in by a voice as slick as sin.

He told me we didn't have much time.

He ordered me naked . . . he ordered me down.

To lay spread eagled, upon the polished bedroom floor.

I took one look at his enlarged state and new this would be flat out rape.

As he started his way towards me . . . grabbing me by the back of my neck.

I kneed him in the groin and jumped the hell back.

He fell and hit his head on the edge of the wooden bed frame.

I ran to him searching for a pulse in vain.

I knew his life was lost . . . I ran from the master's room.

I didn't get far in my plan to escape.

A house servant had discovered his body . . . I was to be hanged.

I had no rights.

Gasping for air as the ropes tightened, around my neck.

I could feel the horse restless beneath me as I began to pray silently.

The horse suddenly lurched forward violently.

The blood rushed to my head.

Breathing exchanged for gurgling instead.

My vision blurred . . . I twitched violently unable to stop.

The rope cutting off my circulation . . . urine pouring from my body in frustration.

All of my senses everywhere at once.

I found the strength to focus, once more on the face of death.

As it kissed my still warm lips . . . promising it would be over soon.

Telling me many slaves lives had ended this way.

Screaming I woke up with a start . . .

My throat was raw and my legs were spread apart.

I could still feel the rope burns, upon my flesh.

I breathed forth a sigh of relief that God had taken mercy on me.

Allowing me to be born free, instead of being born a slave.

Dangling lifeless from my master's tree . . .

"The Realization Of Those That No Longer See . . ."

Every morning I raise my head, is another morning tears should be shed.

As I look into the mirror at none other then me.

I was born a product of poverty.

Here I stand a little over five feet tall.

I am a black woman.

Blessed over all.

I get to be the realized dream of ancestors past that only caught a gleam.

Of the life freedom and the right to be.

I am the realization of those that no longer see.

A people that knew true misery.

Their remains have long since turned to dust.

But what's this?

A heartbeat . . . followed by millions.

Holding vigil in my soul.

My ancestors haven't died in vain.

For clearly parts of them must remain, within the vessels of my being.

I am and I will always be.

The realization of those that no longer see . . .

"The Land Of Self Worth . . ."

The land of self worth in which we reside.

Measuring who we are by how many materialistic things we can buy.

Feeling the weight of the world falling heavily, upon your brow.

Wondering how much do you need to be accepted now?

Will enough ever be enough?

Can I ever call their bluff!

The land of self worth is not a pleasant place to be.

People are looked down upon, like different types of pedigree.

There used to be a time where the amount of money you made, wasn't the deciding factor that ruled.

You were judged by your personality and the things you do.

Now the status quo has changed.

If you are not making six figures a year, your nobody.

Going nowhere.

The land of self worth in which we all reside.

Measuring who we are never mind what's on the inside.

Feeling the weight of the world, the bite of society.

No matter what you may have achieved, your always feeling something pulling at your sleeve.

You need more to prove you are worthy of the grain.

When it's time for you to die, the process is the same.

    Name on the tombstone. Body in the grave.

    Doesn't matter if you were a English king or a Georgia slave.

All of your worldly possessions are scattered in the wind.

    Doesn't matter the sights you have seen.

Doesn't matter if you were dirty or clean.

    What does matter is your spiritual being! ! !

The rich and poor are even once more.

"Running Wolf . . ."

Standing atop of a mountain side . . .

Is a Indian chief filled with honor and pride.

Not knowing what the future may hold.

This Indian chief is beautiful and bold.

Over looking the land that belongs to you and me.

Wondering how much longer his people would be free.

The village in which he has sworn to protect.

In his world where everyone respects.

I don't know what cruel hands of fate, helped decide, help dictate.

Who would be enslaved, who would be free?

Who would suffer to no degree?

Children playing in the wind.

Mothers tending to the chores of their men.

Warriors training for a brand new day.

Elderly ones swatting the mosquitos away.

A life that was fierce.

A lifestyle that died swift.

The enemy coming in many forms . . .

The United States government, prejudice in the faces that vent.

    Rage and hatred for reasons unknown, to much time spent.

Planning the demise of a race.

    That wanted to live in peace.

To have the rights of all men, but it was decided they would be better off deceased.

    The life of a Indian chief.

Some lived for decades, while other lives were brief.

    Fighting for the protection of those they love.

A way of life that was splendid . . . a way of life that has ended!!!

"The Bond . . ."

Holding your daughter in your arms.

Upon giving birth to her, she immediately begins to work her charms, on her mother.

Who can't help but see, a little of herself, coming from every pore.

Not knowing what the world has in store, her little girl will never know.

The heartache of being left alone.

Her beloved daughter will grow up to be a success.

The bond . . . is like no other.

The bond between a daughter and her mother.

It is only as strong and as weak as the hands that tie.

The bond at birth experienced by you and I.

Looking up at the big smiling face, the child instantly senses that there could be no other place.

Where she could get this feeling of worth.

That was presented to her at birth.

She didn't even need to do anything, but arrive.

So that her mother could thrive.

This will surely be a piece of cake, never will my mommy know the ache, of a child gone wrong.

I will love my mommy, for as long as the days belong.

A moment in time that can not be undone, for it is the same as my love.

Burning as brightly as the sun. The bond . . . is like no other.

The bond between a daughter and her mother.

It is as only as strong and as weak, as the hands that tie.

The strings of love that won't let you say goodbye.

"I Want To Belong . . . But Not Really"

I want to belong, but not really.

I crave the kisses of someone true.

I want to belong, but not really.

I want to know that I am missed.

I want to belong, but not really.

I want to be loved, but I feel silly.

I want to belong, but not really.

I want to enjoy the touch of a man.

I want to belong, but not really.

I want to do something worth wild in my life.

I want to belong, but not really.

I want to be strong and independent.

I want to belong, but not really.

I want to think of myself as beautiful.

I want to belong, but not really.

I want to help people.

I want to belong, but not really.

I want to know that my life was not in vain.

I want to belong, but not really.

I have lived my life like a nomad.

I want to belong, but not really.

I find reasons to keep going on.

I want to belong, but not really.

Life . . . death . . . memories . . . time and then nothing is left.

But not really . . .

"Just Existing . . . Then You Die"

Diagnosis No. 144 . . . I do believe you should take a seat for this one.

Studying your health charts that date back to your childhood, checking your vitals, too.

My diagnosis is as such, you have fallen victim to just existing and then you die.

I couldn't believe it, either.

The test results don't lie.

It seems you go through life . . . doing the same old things.

Wake up, go to work, come home and sleep.

Never daring to try something new.

To savor the life that was bestowed upon you.

Your slowly collecting dust, on certain aspects of your mind.

Happiness is something you wish you could find.

You are not alone there are many others just like you.

But . . . there is a cure.

Live your life to the fullest.

Live your life as if you were told you only had twenty four hours, in which to behold, the wonders of life beautiful and bold.

Then you will surely start to see your life, as it was meant to be.

"Check Yourself . . ."

You've been hurt . . . so what is that to me.

    I don't see a isle of blood flowing free.

You can function just as good as before.

    Unless you feel you just can't trust anymore?

If that is the case you are trying to make?

    I understand where your heart began to break.

You think I don't understand your pain.

    I don't need to know the root of it's depth, to know the sun shines brightest, after it rains.

    In this world pain often comes with the lessons in life.

You must understand that after the darkness, there will be light.

    So it would appear that you can't find a man that you trust.

I know the feeling . . . if I had a penny for every man that should be cut free, due to his inability to be honest and not stray.

I would fill up a vault in Ft. Knox everyday.

    I no longer settle for second best.

Those men who try to compromise you . . . it's a test.

There are some men out there worth keeping.

So wakeup women and stop your sleeping.

If you find yourself still attracting and falling for those worse types of men.

Maybe you should check yourself and evaluate things from within.

"Comfort Zone . . ."

Right now . . . where are you?

     Are you in your comfort zone?

A place so predictable progress dare not roam.

     Doing just what you need to get by.

The hell with a dream or a piece of the American pie.

     Only living for the next pay check.

Can't even bother to read a book.

     What the heck! ! !

Only caring about your basic bills and a side order of sex.

     Maybe a new outfit or a club you may want to hit.

All the while talking about your baby mama or baby daddy.

     Never stopping to think about the black pioneers that struggled back in the day.

So that the generations now would be more then ok.

     With the education and a strong mindset, there is nothing we can't accomplish.

Yes! Times are hard . . . I feel it too.

     Maybe you have given up on a life that was meant to be lived to the fullest.

There isn't a race that this is reserved for.

This is for the human race . . .

Right now . . . where are you?

Are you in your comfort zone?

What you settle for is what you get out of life.

If you don't even try, as you look around yourself there isn't much point in wondering why?

"The Pretenders . . ."

Funny how you don't miss someone, until they are gone.

Funny how love was never on my mind . . . just something for movies and songs.

I can't do anything now but just pretend.

We may have had a little something that could have grown.

Not that either one of us would have known.

We were both unprepared . . . maybe a little scared.

So we act as if we never began.

You and I linger in a stance undefined.

No jealous feelings dance around in my mind.

Besides you have long since moved on which is fine by me.

I would never have allowed you and I to really be.

You and I are so different like night and day.

We should have never allowed a ounce of feelings to get in the way.

Instead we crossed those invisible lines and now it's to late.

There is nothing to salvage . . . only misunderstandings.

I wish I could be completely honest with you, but your ego is so demanding.

Your one of those men that believes no woman can turn them down.

Sometimes I still think of you but my thoughts don't make a sound.

Soon the footsteps you left behind, across my heart will start to fade.

For you and I are the pretenders . . . whose hearts will never know pain, because they are so far out of reach, from the world locked away in a safe place we have everything to gain.

"Every So Often . . ."

Every so often I wonder what it would be like . . . to let down my walls and
venture to the other side.

Where those who are not afraid to really live, take life and make it their
slave.

Doing what most of us only dream, while making it seem as easy as
licking icecream.

Molding the world in which we reside.

Setting the standards oh so high.

They are just like you and I.

The only difference is they had the heart and believed.

Most of us never really live before we die.

Imagine a entire life in which you just sip, from the cup of life as it continues
to drip.

Down your chin landing in a pool on the floor.

Never really having the full experience, before you fill your cup up once more.

Just going about the daily ritual.

Never stopping to think what is this magical thing . . . the life I drink?

Taking for granted more will always be there to replenish your cup,
when the last has disappeared.

Did it ever occur to you that you have a life for a reason?

You could have been born a tropical disease, a nightmare without a breeze, a winter cold followed by a sneeze, a wildfire burning the leaves.

Instead you were born a human being.

Granted a incredible life. But do you believe?

"A Prince Amongst Thieves . . ."

In a world where the same men come along.

No dazzle just content to sing you the same song.

You find yourself put off to say the least.

Hiding in search of that well deserved peace.

Needing to find a soul similar to your own.

Your looking for a prince amongst thieves.

One who is ready to claim his thrown.

A man that isn't under the false notion that he must have sex, with a ocean of women to prove his worth.

But a real man that knows he was worth a million since birth.

Is it to much to ask . . . to hope to find a man that is interested in what goes on in my mind?

A man that looks me in the eyes first and checks out my body last.

Finding a prince amongst thieves, it would be easier to find hell through a looking glass.

Than to find a man that can actually pass for what is and what was meant to be, the virtues of a man for me.

In a world where the same men come along, no dazzle just content to sing you the same song.

You find yourself in search of peace, from the men that have been branded beast.

You find yourself not asked to dinner, but are the actual feast.

A prince amongst thieves I would hope to find, as I open my eyes and look about me.

I realize he can only be found in my mind . . .

"Should She Take A Chance On This?"

Once upon a time there was a confused young lady, who didn't know what to do . . .

She lived in an apartment, though not in a shoe.

She had some looks . . . a little whip appeal.

She had a little something she wouldn't allow no man to steal.

Her heart was most valued.

Second to her life that she had lived rather crazy full of strife.

She knew that one day a man would come, along claiming to be the one.

To wine and dine her in the latest style.

To keep her laughing a quarter mile.

To treat her the way a woman(his woman) should be treated.

As she glanced at him not really seeing.

As she listened to him not really believing . . .

Should she try it and take a chance, on this fly by night type of man.

Spinning tales seemingly straight out of Peter Pan.

All she would need is a fairy to appear, so that she would know, if it were pretend or real.

All she would need is to be in his arms one minute to long and he may start to melt her heart of steal.

She wonders if she really wants to know anything about love, before she gets to old . . .

It seems like a hassle . . . it seems like a waste.

Nothing she would ever want to taste.

But to not allow oneself to open up and see . . .

Maybe that is the biggest mistake there could be?

"I Think Of You . . ."

I think of you many times in a day.

    I find myself wishing your presence, in my mind would go away.

I think of you, as my heart skips a beat.

    I think of you as my mind raises it's hands in defeat.

I think of you wondering from where should this go?

    I think of you pondering the thought of how such a attraction could be?

But when I think of you . . . I wish you could just be for me.

    There's a allure of it's own born from nothingness, that came to life.

I think of you . . . with a fondness.

    Even as my words cut, into you like a knife.

I think of you wishing I had nothing to fear.

    I think of you wishing I could have you near.

As I think of you in all of these ways . . .

    I realize I don't know you except to gaze, upon your handsome face.

To actually have the courage to give you a chance.

    I could no more fathom you and I could have a romance.

Your heart has known many, never ready to settle on just one.

    So as I think of you I know we are done, before we even begun . . .

"A Lover's Tryst . . ."

Shining brightly through my bedroom window.

I bask in the sun's warm glow.

Feeling more alive than ever before.

I get up and walk out the door.

Outside I walk upon the dewy grass as the mild wind caresses my flesh.

Tingly sensations overtake me.

I am alive . . . my heart beat speeds at a rapid pace.

Staring across the vineyard I see your face.

Just as strikingly handsome as before.

Your beautiful caramel skin inviting me to come in.

Your perplexing eyes taking me by surprise.

Walking towards you I notice your body's stature rings true.

You have the body of a man whose worked hard to no end.

You look at me in a way that only lover's know.

Falling silently into the grass.

I feel moisture build between my legs.

You caress my every place, once hidden from your adoring face.

We need and want only to be at one with each other for all eternity.

You promise to keep our tryst between just the two of us.

We kiss once more desperately wanting to ignore.

Soon we must part . . .

Our conscious nags at our hearts. We rearrange our clothes as the facade falls apart.

You caress my face once more as you turn to leave.

The illusions of our meeting is broken.

We adore each other in brief moments, as you go about your days, chasing the wind.

I count the long minutes of everyday, until we meet again.

A lover's tryst . . . how much longer shall I greet thee?

"The Man Of My Dreams . . ."

The man of my dreams . . . is a character all his own.

With the sultry looks of a pirate and a ranch for a home.

Filled to the hilt with horses from everywhere, the naked eye could see.

I would love him and if need be he would die for me.

We would be different, yet our love would make us alike.

Not falling victim to the traps that the world has in store.

The art of remaining faithful is not having the heart of a whore.

I would be his best friend and he would be mine.

I won't pretend that we would be Siamese twins.

Engaging in time apart so that we could remain the ultimate in friends.

He would be a tender lover, never boring or self absorbed.

I would cherish him as if he were a rare artifact.

Taking great measures to handle him with care.

Admiring the sharp angles of his body, as I bare my heart and soul so that we could be one.

Trust being overabundant.

The man of my dreams . . . he would be the only one.

"My Heart . . ."

My heart . . .

    Another lover I shall not take.

Place kisses upon my brow.

    Causing my desires to awake.

As you place your hands, upon my body.

    You also caress my soul.

My breasts . . .

    Place kisses upon them.

Allow them not a moments rest.

    Caress my belly . . .

For it flutters anew.

    My body needing and only wanting you.

Take me in your arms.

    Make me a prisoner of your charms.

Caress my darkest, deepest regions.

    Leave no place . . . without the caress of your lips.

Take me to a heavenly place.

    That can only be reached by way of your embrace.

"I"

I feel faint . . . by the very mention of your name.

Your slightest touch, drives me insane.

The personification of beauty.

The intensity of your stare.

Makes me shiver, makes me aware.

That you have to much power, over my sense of being.

I see my reflection, in your eyes.

The utter sincerity took me by surprise.

Melting in a warm honey confection.

I've cast my vote for you since day one, there's no need for re-election.

You are my government, you've brought about peace.

To the jurisdiction known as my heart.

May all war and turmoil cease.

I feel faint . . . but you became my air.

Crisp and vital to my mental care.

When I thought the world had beat me down, you arrived and breathed forth your strength.

While presenting me with a crown, I reside over your heart.

As you keep vigilance over mine.

I feel faint no more, I have found my man.

"Awareness . . ."

You are the breeze that lifts my spirit anew.

    Your touch is always the medicine I crave.

Your kisses keep me from an early grave.

    The light in your eyes reflects the glimmer of the stars.

Your beauty can not be compared, for there is no other like you.

    Your poetry is reflected in everything you do.

Your smile caresses the world with it's glare.

    Only the purest ivory resides there.

Your lips hold the sweetest nectar, ever to be tasted by a human being.

    Your soul is incased in the most beautiful body life has ever seen.

You are my everything, a reflection of a song well sang.

    You roll off my tongue like a evening's rain.

Heaven sent sweet to the pallet and eternal for my soul.

    My beloved in you I exist, never will my love grow old.

"Jamaica . . ."

I met a cool cat, on the way to another day.

Ignoring him seemed to be the only way.

Once out of months of not caring.

I gave in to the cat with the soulful staring.

Eyes so dark . . . you drown from within.

A swagger so strong and pronounced you beg to be let in.

A face so handsome it must be a sin.

For even the wind asks permission, before caressing his skin.

Jamaica used to mean a island under the sun.

Now I think of the accented one.

Who I only knew for a brief moment in time, as I knew he could never be mine.

#3

Inspirational Spiritual
(But do you believe?)

"Experience Of A Lifetime . . ."

Look . . .

But do we really see?

Touch . . .

But how can this be?

Taste . . .

But it's bittersweet.

Life . . .

I'm glad we had a chance to meet.

I've shaken the hand of experience.

I've taken chance out for a bite to eat.

I've caressed destiny right down to his daring feet.

I've kissed the full lips of anguish and held promise in my womb.

Nine months later . . . I gave birth to a healthy mind and spirit anew.

"The Ultimate . . ."

The ultimate is waking up next to the love of your life.

      Being madly in love with your husband or wife.

The ultimate is the freedom to create, it's not to late.

      To expand your mind, like the hands of time.

The ultimate is the touching of people's lives.

      A positive change, to challenge their minds.

To encourage them to want to live another day.

      The ultimate isn't being able to proclaim, I'm a millionaire don't you recognize my name.

      But it's what you do with what the Lord has blessed you with.

To touch the lives of those less fortunate than you.

      The ultimate is being able to say . . . yes I have and now you have too!!!

"The World Feels So Cold . . ."

The world feels so cold.

You have to strain your eyes to find people that seem to really care.

Death common by murder, more often than not.

On the evening news . . . rape, molestation, government officials caught cheating, every evil deed that can be done.

Will be done under the slowly recanting sun.

No one is safe . . . no one untouchable.

It's getting colder.

I feel the ice coldness around my lips.

The evil is bolder as Satan counts his shortened time on his fingertips.

The heart of men corrupted.

Your heart whispers evil and you go right along, until every station in your mind is tuned into that corrupted song.

The world feels so cold . . . basic humanity seems doomed.

But wait . . . this time was seen well before man was redeemed by the blood of Christ.

If you except the gift of salvation life may still be hard for a season, but you will have Jesus as your anchor.

"What Do You Really Want?"

What do you really want out of a life that seems to fly by?

One minute your born the next you die.

Do you desire riches?

Do you desire fame?

Why is it so important for people to remember your name?

Slaving hard at work for years, before you can retire.

Trying to squeeze everything be it good or bad into a life that is due to expire.

Spent like a twenty dollar bill rather quickly, without a damn thing to show.

Why not try investing in something that doesn't fade with time?

Invest in a God that loves you and a Savior(Jesus) that died for you and I.

On Judgment Day no favorites shall be played.

It doesn't matter if you were a famous entertainer, sports hero or highly paid.

I'm not saying don't prepare and enjoy the blessings of life, while you are here.

But consider forever . . . you can be the one to decide where?

"Where Do I Stand???"

Where do I stand?

My mind, body and soul demands . . .

Spreading myself thin to sin.

My mind knows what I have to do, but my body often wins.

I should be serving God as if "Judgment Day" were near. (It is.)

Quiet echoes through time and space.

One day I hope to hear a trumpet sound and be on my way.

As I struggle with my walk as a believer.

This thing called the rapture is real, yet undefined.

Many shake of the thoughts of heaven and hell.

Explaining their version of why we exist.

Ignorance being their eternal bliss.

No amount of bending the bible or science in the world, will save your soul.

Accepting Jesus is the only way.

You don't want to find out to late that your lack of belief and your rights were wrong.

In a place called hell . . . thinking Jesus why didn't I except your gift of salvation, as Satan makes a eternal toast to you lifting his glass of damnation!!!

"Better Now Then Later . . ."

Better now then later . . . is something I heard a lot as a child.

   This saying also applies now.

Putting off what you can do today . . . tomorrow can lead to a lot of sorrow.

   To the backslider or the worldly one that doesn't have a relationship with God.

Go ahead . . . act as if you don't know what I am talking about.

   Stall . . . you will think back to this moment for the rest of your life.

Eternity is promised to you and I.

   The thing is deciding where it is going to be.

Heaven is real.

   Hell it's real too.

Your ignorance is no longer a valid excuse.

   One day we will be held accountable for our decisions of late.

STOP! ! !

   Don't tell me you thought you could bribe your way into those pearly gates?

All the good deeds in the world won't get you in . . .

   Jesus is the key.

Try him in the lock of salvation.

Accept him as your Lord and savior.

There is a mansion with many rooms.

There is a place waiting for you.

It's up to you to decide in which residence you wish to spend eternity . . .

"He Was There . . ."

I haven't lived a life one would be proud of . . . having had my fair share of sexual encounters and one night stands.

Never loving myself enough to wait and place it all in "God's" hands.

He was there . . . even when I was homeless, on the streets needing a place to stay and warm food to eat.

When strangers looked at me the way a dog would a juicy bone.

Or the way the rich would look down their nose at a poor man, in search of a loan.

He was there . . . even when I was stealing from stores, like there was no tomorrow.

Burying deep any form of sorrow.

Trying to make it in a world of pimps, whores, drug addicts, cutthroats and thieves.

A life that wasn't suited for me.

Setting myself up to meet death, before my time.

If not by catching aids than by catching a knife, in my spine.

"God" watched over me even when I didn't watch over nor love myself.

Slowly allowing each sin to take away another one of life's precious breaths.

Always wondering why I could never be the woman who had respect and the decent man waiting for me at home.

I know now that I set into cycle a vicious chain of events.

I vow to try with every breath . . . for everyday that I have left, to learn from my past so as to not repeat it.

"Suicide Watch . . ."

Pushing a small canoe out, into the quiet lake . . .

My belly starts to give me a severe ache.

Hunger pains of not eating right.

Reality walking into my sight.

Having never accomplished, anything worth my wild.

I've decided to end my life here and now.

I am every young girl and boy.

I am a reflection of both good and bad.

Looking into my face you'll see someone's mom or dad.

I am indistinguishable in a crowd.

I've tried drugs just to do something in style.

I've robbed stores for food to eat.

I've stayed with men just for a place to rest my feet.

I've beat up women for reasons unknown.

I've killed in a moment of rage.

Hidden the body in a shallow grave.

I've walked the streets of the city.

Where because of my badge people looked up to me.

I've saved lives in the emergency room.

By knowing which vital organ to cut through.

I've been dating the same woman for over a year.

I told her I loved her then disappeared. I've given birth to a bouncy baby boy.

Whose father has left me for a younger toy.

I've sworn into high offices around the world.

If they only knew the damage I could do . . .

Given the right time and the right place.

I could ruin lives and not leave a trace.

I am all these things and more . . .

The prostitute.

The pimp.

The doctor.

The whore.

The king.

Whose marriage is no more.

Every person no matter the status, in their life.

Finds themselves feeling the agony . . . the bite.

Of this world falling heavily, upon their souls.

Wanting to just find a way out of this hell hole.

The answer that you seek isn't in DEATH.

But GOD! ! !

"Sometimes You Have To . . ."

The world has enough evil revolving through open doors.

Doors you and I have left open, while tending to other chores.

Wanting to give one's life some fresh air.

We allowed the enemy entrance and he dared, to violate our home in which we reside.

Robbing us of our soul and pride.

When we find ourselves drained of hope, sometimes you have to call upon the Lord's name.

You may think it's in vain, but the Lord hears and sees all that you do.

Sometimes even allowing satan to test you.

You may think you are all alone in this world.

Just know that God loves you, above all of his creations ever made.

You're his pride and joy.

God loves the sinner, but hates the sin.

Sometimes you have to allow God in . . . into your heart.

Mesmerizing your soul.

Allow God to redo you from head to toe.

One day you'll look into the mirror and see that God was with you from the time you were conceived.

To the time you fell on your knees . . . praising the Lord our God for all that he did for you.

Wiping away those tears of sin.

Showing you that you don't have to lose, but can win.

Nothing is guaranteed in life, but God's love and mercy.

One day you'll look into the mirror and see . . . you're a new creature in Christ.

Your past will be history.(Do you believe?)

"Reflections Of The Lord . . ."

Reflections of the Lord . . . beauty beyond compare.

Please allow Jesus to take you there.

Majestic streams of forgiveness, gleam from the Lord's eyes.

That never seem to stray from you or me.

Loving us utterly and completely.

Reflections of the Lord . . . beauty beyond compare.

The Lord doesn't want us to suffer, but to be made aware.

That he is Lord of Lord and King of King's.

That if we trust and believe in him utterly and completely.

There is nothing that can't be accomplished through Christ Jesus who strengthens me . . .

"Upon Wanting Companionship . . ."

The Lord found he no longer wished to be . . . alone.

Going on about his usual days.

Talking to all of the angels, as they continued to praise.

The Lord our God for all of his magnificent ways.

He decided that it was time to try something new.

He had his work cut out for him, but then again he always enjoyed a challenge or two.

Creating everything from galaxies to man.

Glancing over at his beloved son . . . Jesus.

Knowing all was going according to plan.

Looking down to earth God couldn't help but see.

Eve conversing with a snake slithering in a tree.

Shaking his head . . . God already knew.

Eve would fall into a fleshly sin, by listening to a fallen angel's lies called Satan.

She allowed him to win.

It's the same as saying to God I could care less about being your friend.

Sure God you gave me life, but this magical serpent will give me the knowledge of wrong and right.

Upon wanting companionship . . . God already knew that his work was cut out for him.

Then again he always enjoyed a challenge or two.

"God Spared No Expense . . ."

God spared no expense when he made me . . . for when I was a child I was as cute as could be.

Having a fair share of innocence, with a touch of sin gleaming, in my eye.

God blessed the child . . . as my mom spanked my behind.

I was never fast in the pants as a child growing up, even though I had a curious mind, about sex like a little pup, who stumbled head first, into a glass of wine.

Ignoring temptation most of the time, yet falling knee deep into sinful crimes.

I knocked on the door of common sense, who used to be a good friend of mine.

When common sense answered the door I screamed out without thinking "Where have you been, you were not supposed to leave me?"

I turned my back for a minute and you were gone.

I've known my fair share of sex still innocent to all the rules, like a cub in the wild.

Which didn't keep me from exploring, with a grin as I discovered the truth wearing my facade of a smile.

I like many others had lost my way, like a kid on a swing who had stopped to play.

Not meaning to get distracted, but not knowing when to say when.

Life pushed my swing to high . . . stupidity made me think I had no choice, but to ride it out to the end.

At least stay on until it slowed down so that I could jump off clean, except I did manage to get a scrap or two.

I always knew life was mean . . .

God spared no expense when he made me.

From the times I was on the streets, without so much as a dime.

To the crazy wild nights, at the clubs for to long of a time.

When I was so out of it I only remember bits and pieces of, the zig saw puzzle that was my life.

After the dawn of a new day of sinful behavior and grown up child's play.

Toying with sex and alcohol was like meat on the table of life, that I became hungry for, so I feasted upon it.

Satan knows my weak spots, he has had time to study.

That's why I am so blessed that "God" continued to love me . . .

He knew one day I would wake from my lucid dream, of sin being fun like eating cake and ice cream.

God knew one day I would yearn for a better life.

That from his table I would yearn to eat, to taste his spiritual meat.

I have so far in which to go, but I must not give up for this I know.

That my life was meant to be so much more.

God spared no expense when he made me.

For he saw everything I was yet to be . . .

"Don't Stop Your Not In The Clear!!!"

For every step I take forward . . . I stop as if I'm in the clear.

I stop to catch my breath . . . I stop to shed a tear.

Allowing Satan time to catch up and pull me to the rear.

For every sin that you believe you are on your way to conquer.

For every temptation you may feel no longer poses a threat.

Two or three are hiding on the side waiting to take you off guard and beat down what little spiritualism you may have left.

You are never over that mountain, for a avalanche is always waiting to fall.

You have never really conquered the castle, for a king and queen still reside in the main hall.

In this world where milk and honey may be sort after, some of us prefer tea.

Every time we find ourselves weakening to temptation, that temptation was especially catered for you and me.

We can't continue to make it so easy for Satan to help us lose our way.

God posts new road signs and maps for us nearly everyday.

All we must do is look and we shall find.

Ask and we shall receive.

Try to resist temptation a little more each time, so as to not cause the Holy Spirit to grieve.

We need to pray a little bit longer, so that we can be a little bit stronger, for the next attack.

Don't stop your not in the clear . . . I can speak from personal experience. I have lost track of the amount of times I have backslid to this day.

I pray to be able to be strong, so that I will be able to last longer, than a radio edited song.

I want the heavens to rejoice, with the angels singing . . . "That's another one for us Lord."

Laughing at how Satan up and ran.

There is a all out bulletin to all saints . . . . hear.

Don't Stop Your Not In The Clear! ! !